# ALASKA'S Sleeping Beauty

## MINDY DWYER

little bigfoot
An imprint of Sasquatch Books | Seattle

Manufactured in China by Midas Printing
International Ltd. (Hong Kong), in December 2013

Published by Little Bigfoot, an imprint of Sasquatch Books
18 17 16 15 14          9 8 7 6 5 4 3 2 1

Editor: Gary Luke
Project editor: Michelle Hope Anderson
Illustrations: Mindy Dwyer
Design: Sarah Plein

Library of Congress Cataloging-in-Publication Data
is available.

ISBN: 978-1-57061-872-7

Sasquatch Books
1904 Third Avenue, Suite 710
Seattle, WA 98101
(206) 467-4300
www.sasquatchbooks.com
custserv@sasquatchbooks.com

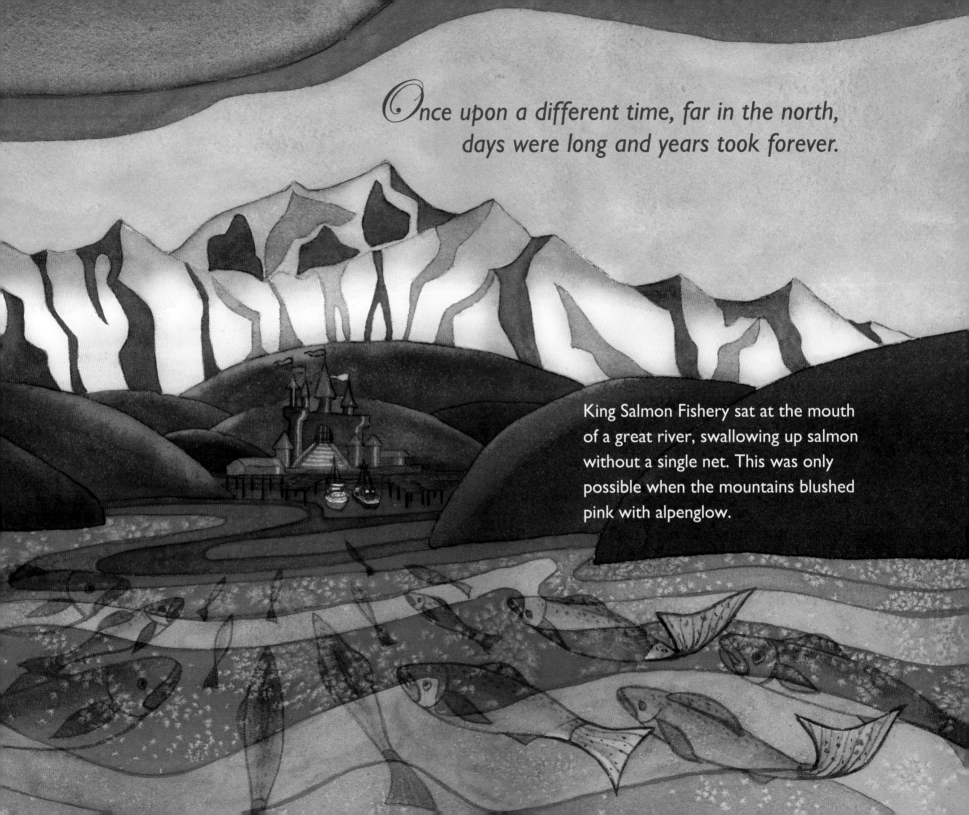

*Once upon a different time, far in the north, days were long and years took forever.*

King Salmon Fishery sat at the mouth of a great river, swallowing up salmon without a single net. This was only possible when the mountains blushed pink with alpenglow.

"My Queen," the King said, his loud voice quaking
the palace, "you are golden as wildflower honey."

"And your heart, my King," the Queen spoke softly,
"is as big as a whale's."

Together they said the words as they did every day,
"Ah, but if only we had a child."

One evening the Queen went down to the dock and dipped her toes in the icy water. A shiver ran up her spine.

In the Far North, just before the midnight sun slips below the horizon, there is a quick flash of green light.

That night, just at that moment, a salmon popped out of the water and said, "My Queen, there will be a child in the kingdom this spring. Call her Alyeska and I will watch over her. I promise."

The salmon swam away before the Queen could say anything.

The Queen grew round with child, and the King was so jolly that his voice just got louder and louder. "Let's have a birth-day celebration! We'll invite the whole kingdom!" he boomed.

"Invite the elders to sit at our table," sang out the Queen, "so they may share their wisdom to help our child grow up."

"Cook," bellowed the King, "stir us up a vat of salmon chowder!"

*Oh, dear,* thought the Queen, remembering the salmon that had visited her. Well, she thought, *if he speaks the future, surely he could swim out of a net and not wind up in the chowder!*

"Baker, bake us a dozen sourdough bread bowls for the elders!" the King said loudly, and the whole palace shook like an earthquake.

"Extra-large, heart-shaped bowls, please," added the Queen sweetly.

Just as salmon swim great distances upriver, news of the birth spread far and wide to the Queen's oldest sister, who thought, *Ugh, all this happiness makes me sick! I can't stand it!*

She was the most miserable, wicked sister. Nothing was ever good enough and she was never happy. In fact, she loved being unhappy. She made jam from poison berries called doll's eyes.

Would *you* invite her to your party?

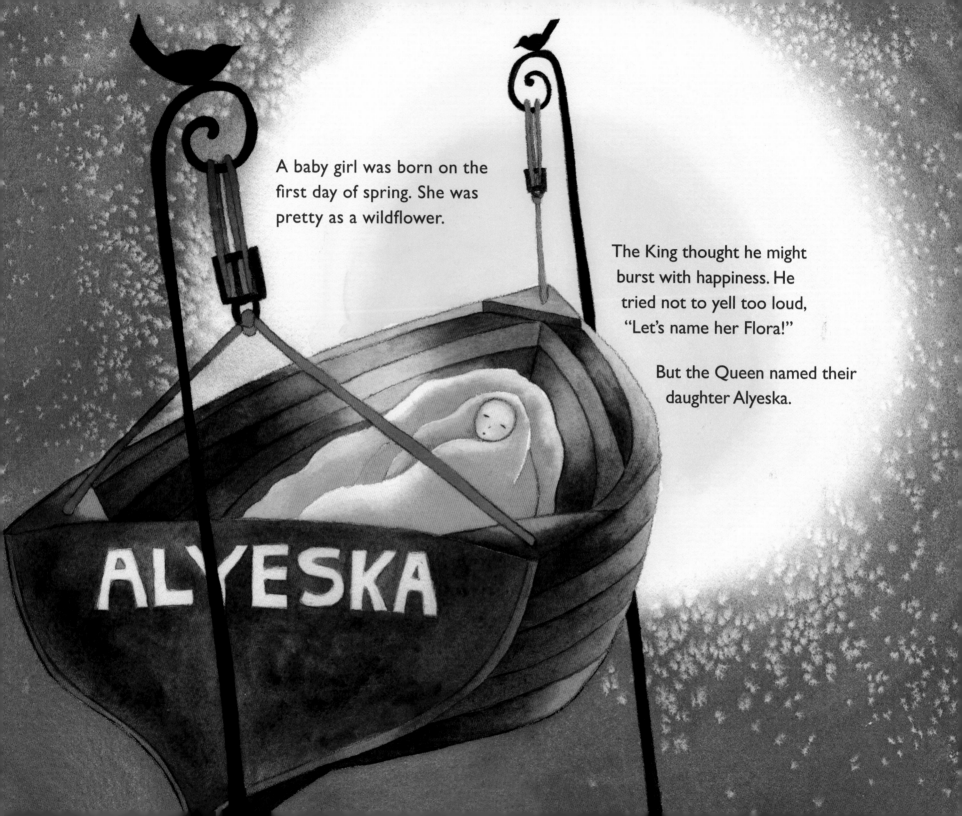

A baby girl was born on the first day of spring. She was pretty as a wildflower.

The King thought he might burst with happiness. He tried not to yell too loud, "Let's name her Flora!"

But the Queen named their daughter Alyeska.

ALYESKA

On the day of the celebration, the palace was packed full of people. The first to speak was the King's mother. "My granddaughter shall one day know love," she said as she gently swaddled the baby in a blanket spun of sunlight.

A teacher placed a towering stack of books next to the cradle for the gift of knowledge.

Next, a hunter spoke of courage, and presented a thick bear-hide rug.

"My gift to the young lady is patience," said a weathered old sled runner from high in the mountains who brought a frisky sled-dog pup.

A mountain climber gave her a glass crystal that reflected colored light and said, "Trust in things that you cannot see, but believe to be true."

A miner said, "Persistence means you must never give up," and gave the child a rock laced with gold.

A lumberjack said, "Always be light of heart," and he laid a necklace on the growing pile of gifts.

This went on and on until there were eleven gifts.

Now, when a baker bakes a dozen, he always bakes thirteen, not twelve. And so, there were thirteen guests at the table set with thirteen freshly baked bread bowls. Even the King did not recognize the uninvited guest until she banged her fists on the table, cackled, and then said . . .

"When the girl grows up, she will choke on a salmon bone and die! How about that!?"

Everyone jumped up out of their seats and ran in circles, wondering what to do.

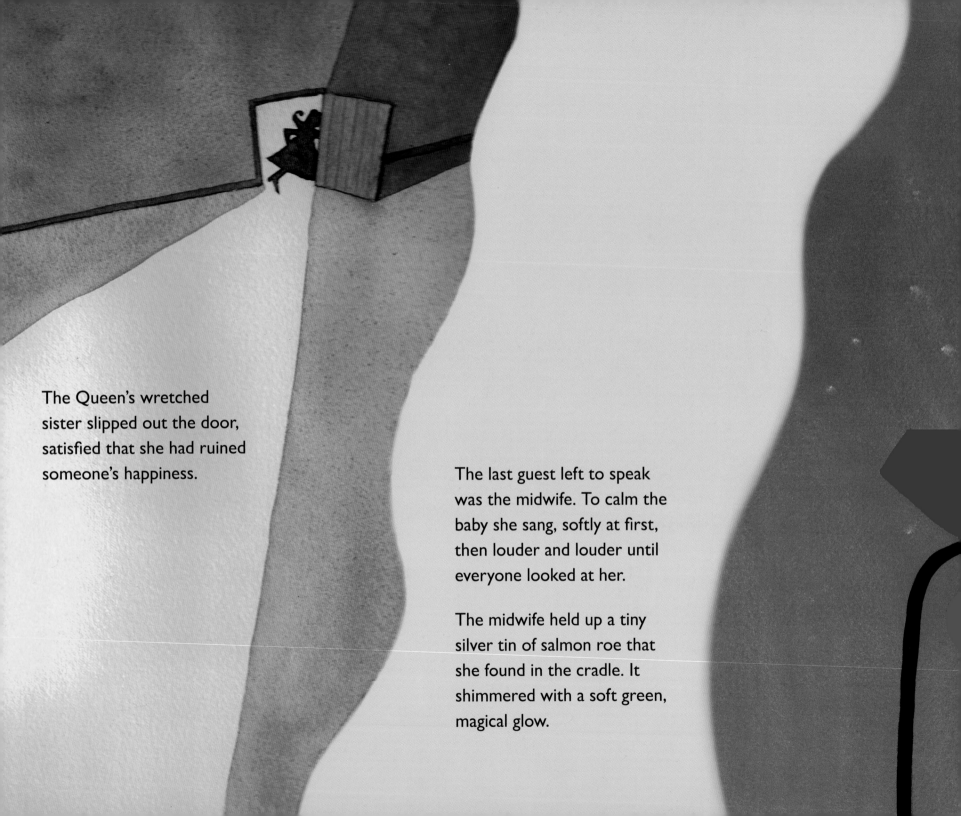

The Queen's wretched
sister slipped out the door,
satisfied that she had ruined
someone's happiness.

The last guest left to speak
was the midwife. To calm the
baby she sang, softly at first,
then louder and louder until
everyone looked at her.

The midwife held up a tiny
silver tin of salmon roe that
she found in the cradle. It
shimmered with a soft green,
magical glow.

"Alyeska will live!"

Then she reached into her bag and stuffed dried passionflowers into a little pillow. "When she chokes on a salmon bone, Alyeska will sleep for a long, long time on this dream pillow but wake up when her time is right."

To protect his dear little daughter, the King said to his kingdom,
"Remove all fish from the menu! The girl is forbidden to go near
the cannery and she must never hear of this!" He spoke so loudly
that little bits of stone fell from the castle walls.

The child grew into a kind-hearted and brave girl unaware of the curse.
Her eyes were blueberry blue and her hair was Copper River red. She
always did as her mother told her and slept on her dream pillow, filled
with new passionflowers each passing year.

One afternoon, the King and Queen made ready for the maiden voyage of their new salmon boat. Before they set sail, the Queen said to her daughter, "Be careful, and above all, stay away from the cannery."

Alyeska was tired of so many rules and wandered off into the forest. She always carried the tiny salmon tin in her pocket. The roe had long dried up into hard little balls like glass that made a *clickety-clackety* sound when she walked.

On the path she saw a fallen baby bird. Placing it back in its nest, Alyeska imagined being a mother someday. She thought about her own mother, but then . . . she smelled something.

It was different. It was wonderful. It was smoky and deep
and its sweet scent lured her farther into the forest.

Deep in the dark shade of the trees, Alyeska saw a woman working over a smoky fire. "What is this?" she said to the woman, who was cutting long, thin strips and draping them over forked branches. "It smells delicious!"

"You must try it," the woman said, and handed her a piece of smoked salmon. Alyeska had never ever tasted such a satisfying melt-in-your-mouth flavor.

"It's sweet and savory at the same time. It's smoky!" she said and laughed out loud.

As she
laughed, a
small bone
caught in
her throat
and she fell
dead asleep.

At that instant, everyone
in the kingdom fell asleep.

The King and the Queen,
all of the mothers
and all of the fathers,
the cooks, the fishermen,
the canners and the packers,
the animals in the forest . . .
everything in the kingdom stopped.

In the ashes of stillness, fireweed began to grow, blooming higher and higher until it covered the entire kingdom. Fireweed petals spiraled up to the top, marking time while the rest of the land stood still, waiting for the special day Alyeska would wake up again.

News of a princess asleep in the forest traveled far like a fluffy fireweed seed on the wind, and many young men searched for her.

One sunny day a young man came tromping through the forest. His father owned King Crab Fishery, which made him a prince. But he was much more interested in panning for gold and that is just what he was doing when he discovered the magnificent fireweed. The radiant flowers towered high over his head.

"Wow," he said, "I have never ever seen fireweed like this!" His eyes took a long drink of the crazy color, bright as liquid fire. Slowly, the petals began to part a path for him to follow. He entered through the fireweed fence and followed around and around and around until . . .

there she was, in a bed of flowers, a sleeping beauty.

He held her hand and kissed it.
She woke up. "Oh!" she gasped,
and swallowed the salmon bone
that had been caught in her throat
as she slept. "Who are you?"

"My name is Will," said the Prince,
"and I'm looking for gold."

Together they wound around
the puzzling path of fireweed
that opened and closed in a giant
maze. The little salmon tin shook
in her pocket, *clickety clackety.*

"What's that sound?" he asked.

"My lucky charm," said Alyeska.
"I've had it for as long as I can
remember."

When she opened the tin they
saw glowing green candies!
"Candy?" she said. "Sweet!" The
salmon had kept his promise to
watch over Alyeska.

"We'll retrace my steps," Will said. "Let's think our way through this."

Then with a lightness of heart, Alyeska took him by the hand and said, "No, Prince Will, follow me." With every step he knew he would follow her anywhere.

# Then the whole kingdom woke up!

The King and the Queen, the animals in the forest, all the mothers and the fathers woke up. The fishermen, the cooks, the canners, the packers, and everyone else woke up.

The only one who didn't wake up was the one who loved to make people unhappy, who made jam with doll's eyes, who sent curses to babies and served smoked salmon with bones in it!

A feast began immediately. The King made fireweed honey wine, and the cook made his best salmon chowder ever. He also made salmon cakes, salmon steaks, grilled salmon, and lox. The baker baked thousands of bagels.

Alyeska learned how to catch, smoke, and can salmon. She learned to make a good chowder and, most importantly, how to debone a salmon safely.

Alyeska married the Prince and they were happy in their days together. They named their son Coho, future King of King Salmon Fishery.